THE MIXED-UP
MONSTER

Adapted by Ximena Hastings

Ready-to-Read

Simon Spotlight

New York   London   Toronto   Sydney   New Delhi

SIMON SPOTLIGHT
An imprint of Simon & Schuster Children's Publishing Division
1230 Avenue of the Americas, New York, New York 10020
This Simon Spotlight edition December 2019
TM & © 2019 Sony Pictures Animation, Inc. All Rights Reserved.
For information about special discounts for bulk purchases, please contact
Simon & Schuster Special Sales at 1-866-506-1949 or business@simonandschuster.com.
Manufactured in the United States of America 1119 LAK
10 9 8 7 6 5 4 3 2 1
ISBN 978-1-5344-5714-0 (hc)
ISBN 978-1-5344-5713-3 (pbk)
ISBN 978-1-5344-5715-7 (eBook)

Hank and his friends are in the cafeteria at Hotel Transylvania. Hank is happily stuffing worm fries into his mouth when Pedro takes Hank's arm.

Pedro uses Hank's arm to scratch
his back!
"Dude, I was using that," Hank says.
"You guys really have to stop this."

"Stop what?" asks Mavis.
"This!" shouts Hank, looking at
his missing arm.

"You use my hands to climb ladders. You use my legs to dance!" Hank says.

"Why do I have to be a monster that comes apart all the time? I would give anything to be in one piece," Hank says sadly.

"I had no idea you felt that way,"
Mavis says.

"We promise not to do it anymore,"
Wendy agrees.

"Yeah, pinkie swear," Pedro says, as he steals Hank's pinkie finger.

"Maybe there is a way to keep you from coming apart, Hank!" Mavis exclaims.
"Get all the magnets, paper clips, and tape that you can!"

Hank and his friends get to work.
Hank lies down on a table,
looking nervous.

Mavis and Wendy start taping
Hank's scars together.
"Do you really think this is
going to work?" Hank asks.
"Of course it is going to work.
Tape is really strong,"
Mavis says.

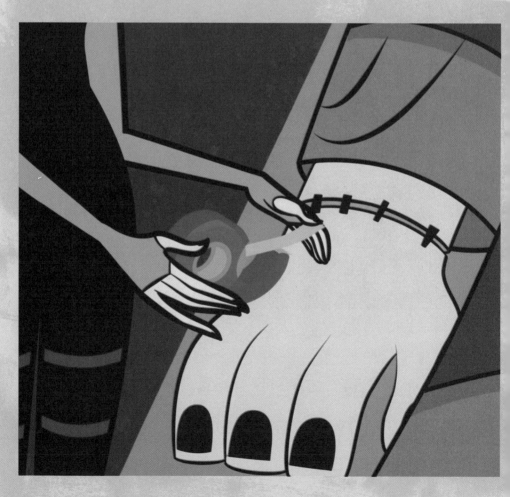

"Just wait until you see it!
Okay, Pedro, tilt Hank to the
mirror!" Mavis orders.

Hank pulls on a switch to
tilt the table up but goes too far
by mistake!

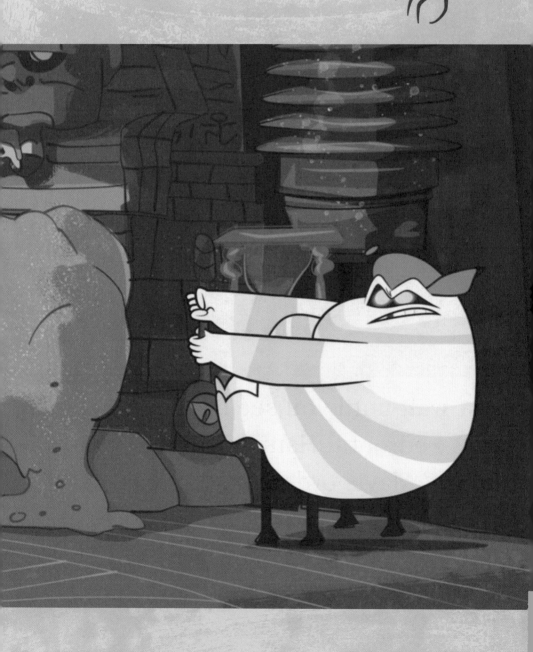

The table is lifted up into a
hole in the roof.
"Hank!" they all scream.
It is too late.
Hank gets zapped!

When the table comes back down,
Hank looks very different . . .

Mavis, Wendy, and Pedro
try to pull off Hank's arms,
but nothing happens.
"Holy rabies!" Mavis exclaims.
"Hank, you are a human boy!"

Hank does some tests around
the hotel.
No matter what he tries, he still
stays all in one piece!

"How are you feeling Hank?"
Mavis asks.
"I feel alive! Alive!" Hank says.
"I have gone from monster to human!"

Aunt Lydia hears Hank.
"A human in the hotel?" she shrieks.
Most monsters are scared of humans,
and the monsters at the hotel start
to panic.

Aunt Lydia forces Hank to leave
the hotel.
"Aunt Lydia, please!" Mavis begs.
Wendy starts crying.

"Thanks for the love, guys,
but this is a hotel for monsters,"
Hank says.
"Hank, you belong here with us,"
Mavis tells him.

"You will always be my friends, but
I have to go be with the other
humans now," Hank says.
He takes his trunk and leaves
the hotel.

It is not long before Hank meets a human named Donald Cartwright! Donald invites Hank to play games with his family.

They play hangman,
they arm-wrestle, and more.
Hank has so much fun.
"I love being human!" Hank says.

Back at the hotel Mavis and the others learn Hank is in danger of being stuck as a human forever! "We have to save Hank!" Wendy says.

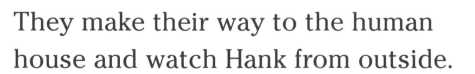

They make their way to the human
house and watch Hank from outside.

Inside, Hank wants to help
the human family with things
like dancing.
He wants to help the monster way,
but it does not work.
His legs do not just come off
like they used to!

Hank misses being a monster.
"I miss my friends, and I miss my
old life. Even my scars are fading,"
he says. "What am I going to do?
I do not want to be a human forever."

Suddenly, Mavis has a great idea
to save Hank.
"If Hank is in the house, and the
house is zapped like he was,
everything should go back to normal
because . . . science!" Mavis says.

Mavis uses Wendy and Pedro to create a kite . . . and the house gets zapped!
Hank goes back to being a monster!

Back at Hotel Transylvania,
Hank is happy to be home.
"Man, do I feel good!" Hank says.
"I love being myself, and I love
being a monster!" he cheers.